ALTADENA LIBRARY DISTRICT
3 9270 00240 5243

D0852369

On Christmas Eve

BY LIZ ROSENBERG • ILLUSTRATED BY JOHN CLAPP

Brookfield, Connecticut

A NEAL PORTER BOOK

Published by Roaring Brook Press
A division of The Millbrook Press, 2 Old New Milford Road, Brookfield, Connecticut 06804

Library of Congress Cataloging-in-Publication Data
Rosenberg, Liz.
On Christmas Eve / by Liz Rosenberg ; illustrated by John Clapp.
p. cm.
Summary: Unable to reach Aunt Cleo's house on Christmas Eve because of a wild snowstorm, a young boy worries that Santa Claus won't be able to find his family at the motel where they are stranded.
[1. Christmas—Fiction. 2. Santa Claus—Fiction. 3. Snow—Fiction.] I Clapp, John, ill. II. Title.
PZ7.R71894 On 2002
[E]—dc21 2002019951

ISBN 0-7613-1627-2 (trade)
2 4 6 8 10 9 7 5 3 1

ISBN 0-7613-2707-X (library binding)
2 4 6 8 10 9 7 5 3 1

Printed in Hong Kong
First edition

For David who makes it Christmas Eve every night
and for Claudia Jaccarino and her family
who loaned a little Jewish girl Christmas
—L.R.

For Mary—her first book.
—J.C.

It was a long drive to Aunt Cleo's house, but that was all right.

It was Christmas Eve.

We crammed into the car.

My older brother, Adam, complained, and the baby blew bubbles.

I showed her the lit-up houses along the way

It began to snow lightly as we crossed the state line.

Then the storm grew thicker

NE
12

and wilder.

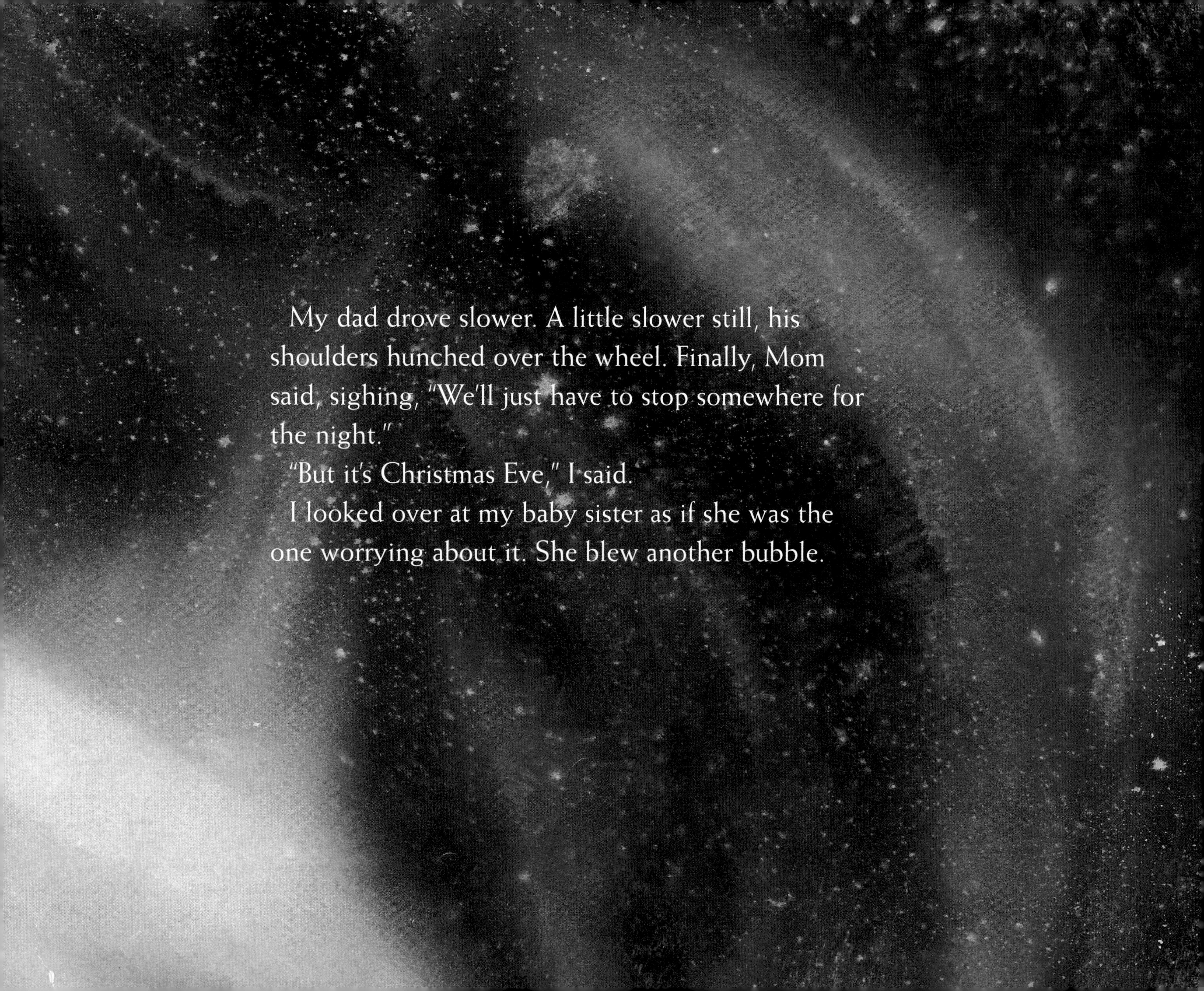

My dad drove slower. A little slower still, his shoulders hunched over the wheel. Finally, Mom said, sighing, "We'll just have to stop somewhere for the night."

"But it's Christmas Eve," I said.

I looked over at my baby sister as if she was the one worrying about it. She blew another bubble.

MOTEL
VACANCY

One of the letters in the motel sign had gone out.

"They don't even have cable TV here! Or a swimming pool!" yelled my brother.

Like we were going swimming in December.

But there was still this one thing. I mentioned it to my mother in a low voice. "There's no chimney—not even a mailbox."

"Santa will find us," my mother said. "He always finds a way."

"Only babies believe in Santa Claus," my brother told me later. We lay in the dark motel room. It didn't feel like Christmas.

All the same, after everyone else had fallen asleep, I hung up our stockings and laid out my last piece of Majic bubble gum and a package of peanut butter crackers. Just in case.

Then I waited by the motel room window. "I wish Santa would come," I whispered.

The glass fogged with the breath of my words. The fog formed a cloud, which grew rounder, larger, silvery, and thin, then disappeared into the air.

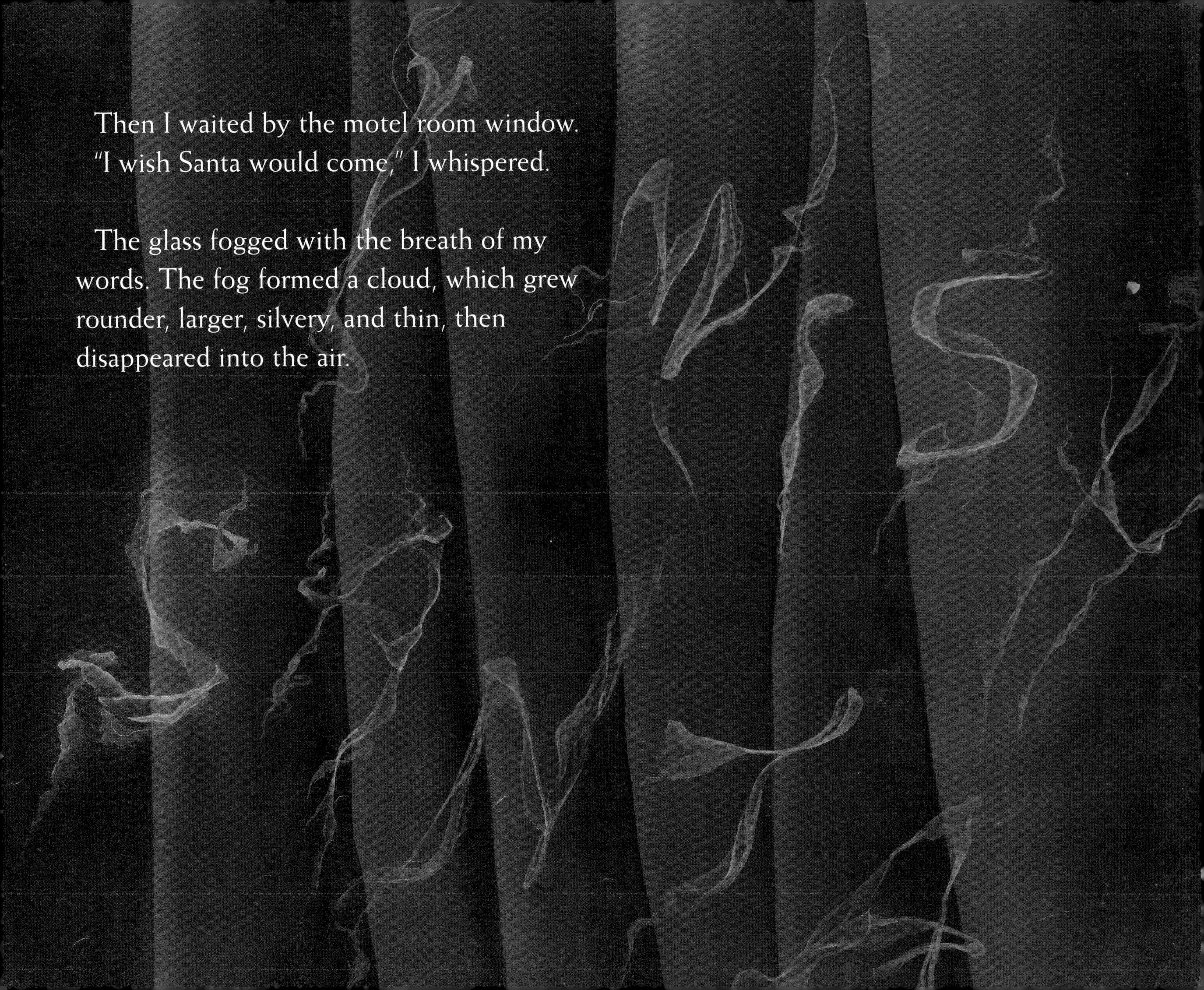

I must have fallen asleep.

Something woke me—what was it? The sound came again, distant ringing, like frogs in summer.

In the sky I saw the faraway blinking lights of an airplane. It had lights strung all over it, like a Christmas tree.

No, it looked more like a strange sort of kite.

A sled!

MOTEL
VACANCY

He looked smaller than I had imagined. And the reindeer looked bigger.

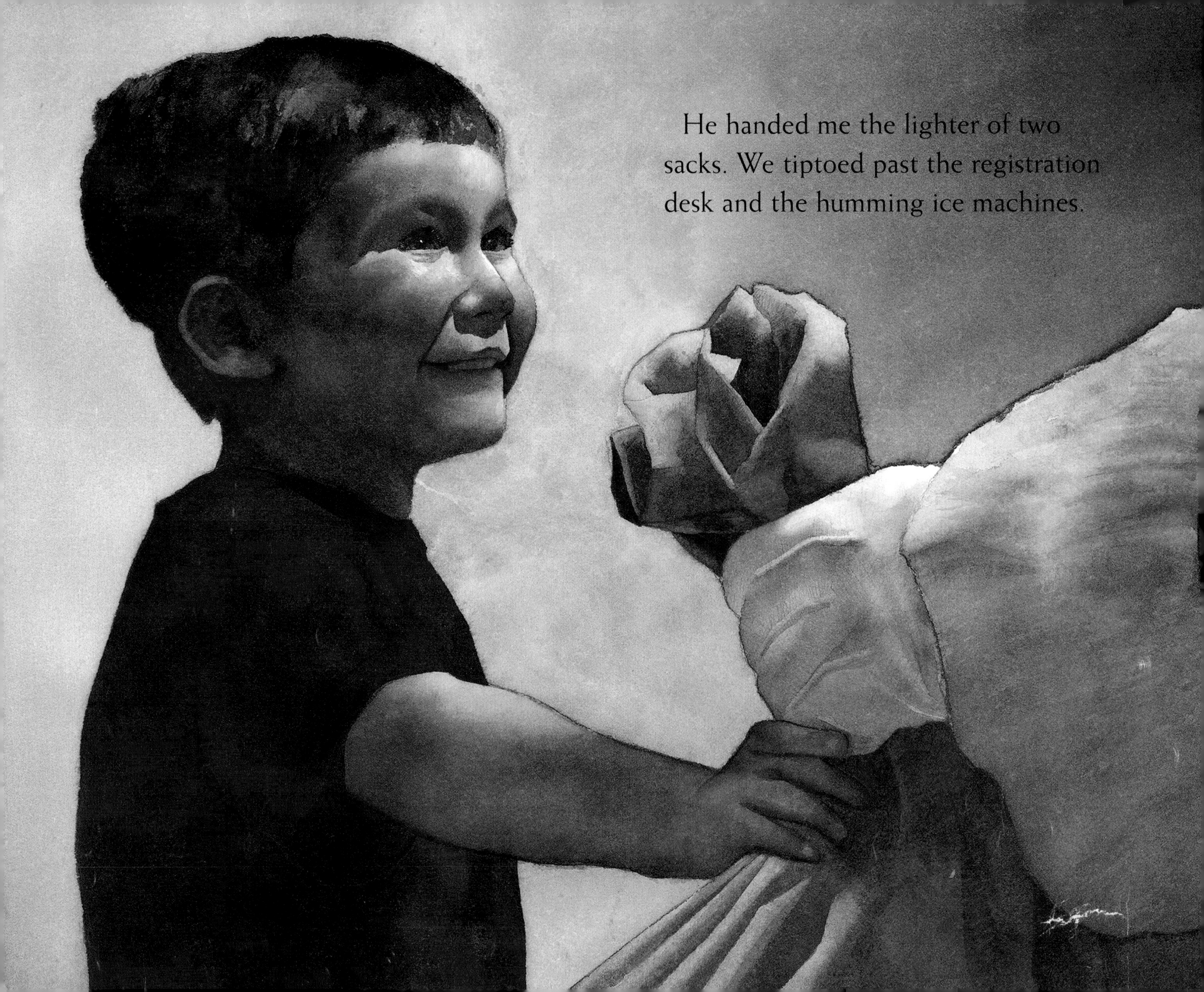

He handed me the lighter of two sacks. We tiptoed past the registration desk and the humming ice machines.

"Thank you," he said.
"I love bubble gum."

FOR CHRISTMAS I WOULD LOVE

IS THERE REALLY A

Back outside, he pointed to the sky.

Then, the reindeer lifted their heads. Swiftly and surely they ran, till with a leap they bounded into the air, then higher, flinging themselves at the sky as if climbing a mountain—and flew, over the broken motel sign

into Christmas morning.

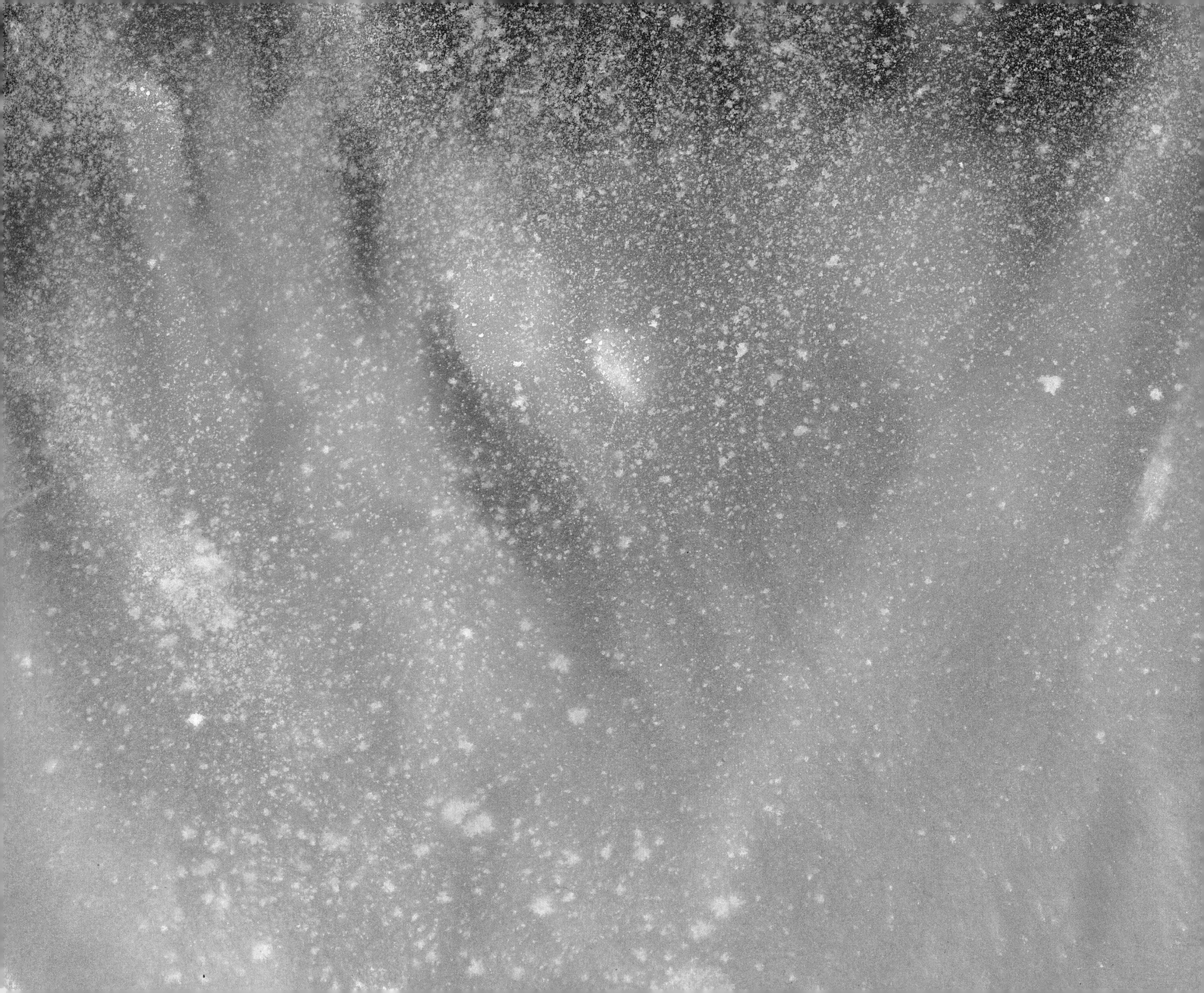